OUT OF
THE DARK

Also by Adèle Geras

OUT OF THE DARK

ADÈLE GERAS

Quercus

First published in Great Britain in 2015 by

Quercus Editions Ltd
55 Baker Street
7th Floor, South Block
London W1U 8EW

A CIP catalogue record for this book is available
from the British Library

PB ISBN 978 1 78429 125 9
EBOOK ISBN 978 1 78429 208 9

10 9 8 7 6 5 4 3 2 1

Printed and bound in Great Britain by Clays Ltd, St Ives plc

Typeset by CC Book Production

FOR HELEN,
who liked reading LILY

Chapter One

My name is Rob Stone and I have no face. I had a face before I went to war but it was shot off. I wear a mask now. The mask is made of thin metal. It's painted to look like a proper face but it's not. It's to cover up where my face used to be.

They try to make the masks look like you, before you were hit, but it's hard to do that. My mask doesn't look like me at all. The only things that remain the same are my mouth and my chin. I was told I was lucky that those had been spared.

I left hospital a few weeks ago. I thought that maybe the captain would stay behind in the ward, but he came with me.

Captain Harry Ashton died in France, but I still see him. He came to sit on my bed when things were bad and the sight of him comforted me. I told no one about him. They would have sent me to a mental ward. They would have said my mind had gone. That's not true. I'm all there, but I see the captain from time to time. He comes back to me. He comes to help me do what I have to do. I haven't done it yet, but I will. I promised myself I would.

When the war started, I joined the army with my friends. We wanted to enlist and have a go at shooting the enemy for king and country. We all said that. We thought it would be a short war. The girls called us heroes and we liked being praised. We were eager to leave for France.

We didn't get that much training. They gave us rifles and told us how they worked. They let us have a go with bayonets, the sharp knives attached to the barrels of the rifles. We spent hours running at dummies. The dummies were stuffed with straw, and we ran up and stabbed them. We did this over and over again. They reckoned it would teach us to run at a man and stick him in the guts. I am glad I never had to do that. I worried about sticking a knife in a real person.

When we went to France, I thought it was going to be like a holiday. We sailed over the Channel and I watched the white cliffs of Dover getting further and further away. We sang songs. We were with our pals. We thought we would come back when the Huns had been beaten. We were sure it would not take long. Huns was our name for the Germans.

But after a bit I began missing my home. I wanted to be back in London with my mother. I longed for my room in the attic of our house. There, the ceiling sloped down above my bed. I had a little window to look out of. I could see roofs and the tops of lamp posts. I could look down at people walking in the streets. At night there were lights in the windows. When a fog came down, it wrapped itself around the street lamps and made the light fuzzy and soft.

Even up in the attic, I could hear the noises from the street. Horse-drawn carriages made the best noise: clip, clop, clip, clop. When I was a little boy I used to lie in my bed and repeat the nursery rhyme 'Ride a cock horse . . .' to myself before I fell asleep.

In France there was a trench, and a hard bed and mud on the floor and the cries of sad men. They, too, had left everything they loved for the first time and were missing home, just like me. Later, after we'd heard the guns and the screams of men torn apart and bleeding, the sounds in the trench changed. We fell into our bunks wishing we could dream of home. More often than not, we woke up shrieking from a nightmare.

Before I went to war I was happy. I had a job at the draper's shop on Essex Avenue. It was owned by Mr Gordon. My mum had worked for him for years, and she put in a good word for me. I never thought I would like making displays of silks and knitting wools for the window, but I did. I liked meeting the ladies. When they came into the shop, they often asked for me.

'Rob, please come and help me choose a ribbon,' they would say. Or, 'I need your help, Rob. What colour fabric shall I get for this frock?'

Mum said, 'They like your big blue eyes, Rob. That's what it is. They like your smile.'

I was good at helping them choose what they needed. My friends Tom, who worked for a grocer, and James, who worked as a butcher's boy, thought it was girly and sissy to serve ladies every day. I think they were jealous. Many of the young ladies who came into my shop, but not into theirs, were very pretty.

When Millie came in to buy a reel of cotton, I liked her at once. I liked her better than any young lady I'd ever seen. What I felt for her was not the same as what I'd felt for other girls. She was very pretty and she liked me. I knew she did, because she came into the shop a lot and always asked for me.

My mum said, 'I think you should talk to her.'

'I do talk to her,' I said.

'You know what I mean. Ask her to meet you in the park. If you go on Sunday, you can listen to the band. I know her mother, Mrs Evans. I've seen her in church. They're good people, I'm sure.'

I didn't ask Millie, even though I wanted to. In the end, she asked me. She came up to the counter, ever so bold, and said, 'I'll be at the bandstand in the park on Sunday, Rob. They play very nicely. Why don't you come along and listen?'

So I did. We sat on a bench near the bandstand and listened to the marches and the waltzes. I didn't hear the music. I just thought about how near I was to her, about how I'd like to hold her hand. I thought about how pink her mouth was. I looked at the way the sun shone through the holes in her hat and made patterns on her skin. I wanted to kiss her. I had to stop myself from leaning over and touching her lips with mine.

After the music stopped we walked along the grey paths in the park. I wished that I could stay walking round the park with Millie for ever.

The sun was low in the sky when we said goodbye. I walked her right up to her gate.

'Will you walk with me again next Sunday?' I asked.

She nodded and said, 'Yes. We had a lovely time, didn't we?'

Then I did it. I leaned over and kissed her quickly on the lips. She leaned closer to me and put her hand in mine. I could feel her warmth through our clothes.

'Oh, Rob,' she said and squeezed my hand. 'I do like you so much!'

I didn't know how to tell her how much I liked her, so I kissed her again. I felt the taste of her on my lips all the way home and all through the night, too.

Chapter Two

I hated the war. There was mud at the bottom of our trenches. The noise of gunfire never stopped for long. It was wet and cold, and I was scared of getting killed. We all were. The only good thing about it was that you were with your chums. Tom and James joined up with me, and so there were three of us.

When we got to France, we went straight to the battlefields. First we drove for miles and then we marched. The food was disgusting. I thought of my mum's fruit cake and groaned. We thought about food a lot. We used to say the names of things at night to cheer ourselves up but it made us feel worse not better.

'Hot buttered toast,' Tom might say.

'Roast beef. And roast spuds. With gravy,' I might reply. I could taste it when I said it.

Our trench was lined with wooden planks. The rain still made mud which came through the gaps in the planks and soaked our boots. Our feet were always damp. I felt cold, wet and stiff most of the time, even in my bunk.

But the worst thing was going over the top. When we heard the order, we had to leave the safety of the trenches. Then we ran. As we ran, the Huns shot at us. They didn't stop shooting, not even for one minute. I could hear the rattle of the guns. I could see my chums running, but I couldn't see who anyone was. You just put your head down and ran towards the enemy lines.

My friend Tom, from the grocer's shop, didn't live very long. I saw his death. I saw him being blown apart. Pieces of his body flew through the air. I saw it. I saw him in bits, with blood spraying out of him and I tried not to see him. I tried to forget this, but I couldn't. I tried to think of him how he was: yellow hair and bright brown eyes and a cheeky look about him. But it was hard. Whenever his name came into my mind, what I saw was his exploding body. The bits and pieces of him flying through the air.

'We'll have to tell his mother,' James said, 'when we get back to Blighty.'

I nodded. I didn't want to think about that. I took out a letter that had come from Millie and read it again. I wanted to write to her but didn't know what to say. I couldn't tell her about Tom. I couldn't find the right words.

The captain was very kind to me when Tom died. His name was Harry Ashton and he was just like one of us. He spoke to us, and seemed to like me better than most. When I woke up at night, sobbing, he'd come and sit by me and talk.

One night, he showed me a picture postcard of his family.

'We had this taken before I left home. This is my wife, Edith, and this is my daughter. She's called Kitty. Catherine, really, but she's Kitty to us.'

His wife was nice-looking and had her hair pulled back in a bun. Kitty, the daughter, wore shiny black boots and a pinafore. There was a doll sitting on a low chair next to her. She was five years old, the captain said. In the picture, Captain Ashton was in uniform and looked brave and handsome. I turned it over and the photographer's name and address were stamped on the back. 'KENTON PHOTOGRAPHERS, 35, Bridge Street, London SE1.'

'I try and write to Edith and Kitty as often as I can,' the captain said. 'But it's hard telling them lies.' He smiled at me. 'They don't want to know how things are here. Not really. I pretend it's all glory and never tell them about the rest.'

I nodded. I had almost stopped writing home. I didn't want to tell Mum how things were. Captain Harry put the postcard back between the pages of a Bible that he'd brought with him. It was kind of him to show me his family, I thought. He was a kind man. I think I would have gone off my head if it hadn't been for him.

We fought. We slept when we could. We cried and wept at night. Almost every day, we ran with our mates over the top. Then, one day, the captain was hit. He died at once and that was a mercy.

'Nothing left to bury,' someone said. 'Blown to pieces.'

I cried more for the captain than I had for Tom, and I felt bad about that.

'Go and fetch his things,' someone said to me. So I put his stuff into a kitbag. When I got to the Bible, before I could think about what I was doing, I stole it. There is no other way of saying this. I wanted the postcard I knew was in it more than I wanted the good book, but I shoved it under my jacket.

Later on, I moved it to a safe place in my own kitbag. I woke up shortly before dawn and took out the postcard and stared at it in the dim light.

The captain, his wife and his daughter. The white lace on his wife's blouse and the white pinafore worn by his little girl seemed to glow in the early light.

Maybe what I did was wrong, but I couldn't help it. I knew what I had to do. I would go and find Edith. I'd find Kitty and tell her what a fine man her daddy had been. I planned to give the postcard back. The Bible was there to stop the postcard being bent out of shape. I hoped the holy words would mean it would be kept safe until I could pass it on to Mrs Ashton.

The captain was dead, but even so I kept seeing him. Once, in the trench, I saw him sitting by a wounded man, putting his hand on the chap's knee. Once, as we marched from one muddy place to another, I was at the back of the line and he was there when I looked round.

Then my face got shot off and he came to me. He was there while I screamed and cried. He sat on my bed in the night, as I burned with pain. He faded a bit when the drugs took hold. For weeks, he was with me. I was moved to a hospital in England and he didn't leave me. I knew he'd stay with me till I did what I'd promised myself I would do. I had to find his family. I had to give them the postcard.

Chapter Three

While Millie and I were walking out, we liked going to the pictures. On a street near her house, beside the canal, there was a film studio called Wonderland.

'They make the films there,' Millie told me, 'right near where we live. Imagine!' She liked the actors and the pretty actresses, and looked at any pictures of them that she could find in the papers. 'I saw one of the dancers getting out of a car,' she said once, sounding excited. I never saw any actors, but I did notice shiny cars driving along the roads sometimes. Still, I liked the moving pictures.

Our cinema was called the Majestic. It was funny to think the people in the films were real men and women, because they were also somehow more than that. They were bigger than us. They were better dressed and better-looking than we were, and they were doing things we'd never do. We loved watching them.

Best of all, it was dark in the Majestic. I could hold Millie's hand and even kiss her. I lived for the moment when the lamps dimmed and I could look forward to the taste of her, and the touch of her. After the film was over, we went outside in a kind of dream. We loved the Majestic. It became the most important place in the world to me.

My face took a long time to heal. I came out of hospital in July 1920, months and months after I first went in. During those months, no one came to see me except Mum, and Millie, once. The first time my mother saw me, she started crying and didn't stop for a long time. In the end she sniffed and said, 'Crying isn't going to help, is it? What can't be cured must be endured. I'll look after you. I don't give a fig what you look like.'

The doctors were very kind. They took trouble to explain everything to me.

'In time,' said Dr Hughes, 'when your face has healed enough, we may be able to . . .'

I waited while he searched for the right words.

He went on, 'We may be able to patch you up a bit. Take skin grafts from different parts of your body. You won't have to wear a mask for ever, you know.'

'But you can't make me look like I did before, can you?' I asked.

'No,' he said. 'Not like you were before.'

'I'll think about it,' I told him. I wasn't sure if I didn't prefer a mask, however strange it looked. At least it was smooth and hard and covered up the raw, red bits of me. 'Patch you up,' Dr Hughes had said, and I could imagine it. My face would be seamed and ridged. It would be criss-crossed with lines of scar tissue, and the scar tissue would never fade. I'd have a face like a map. I would be ugly for ever.

Once I was back home, with my painted metal mask on, my mum set about finding me a job. She wasn't one to fool herself.

'You're not going to be much use in the shop for a bit,' she said. I didn't answer, because she was right. No pretty girls would go up to a monster and ask his advice about dress fabric.

I ate my tea, and my heart felt as if it was sitting in my chest like a lump of lead. I'd seen what happened when I walked through the streets. Most people looked away. Some turned to go into a shop when they saw me coming. Children started crying more often than not. There were some who pointed at me. Others muttered . . . I heard them saying things like,

14

'Shouldn't be allowed,' or, 'Should be locked up away from other people.'

I thought I'd be happy once I was at home, but I wasn't. This was because I had lost Millie. I'd lost her long before, during the early weeks of my stay in hospital. I've tried to forget what happened when she came to visit me that morning, but I can't get it out of my mind. It was the worst thing I'd ever lived through.

Worse than having my face shot off? Well, the pain was in a different spot, that's all. The drugs that helped with that agony didn't touch this sort of hurting. I had small sponges on sticks by my bed so I could dampen my mouth to make my lips less dry and sore. There wasn't anything that could make my heart hurt a little less.

This is what happened. I've tried to forget it but I can't. Millie came into the room where I was lying in my bed. She burst into tears and nothing I could say or do could stop them.

'Millie,' I said. 'It's me. Really. It's me under the bandages. Do you remember what I looked like? I might not look like that now but I'll be . . .'

'What?' Millie cried out. 'What will you be? Oh, I can't bear it, Rob. I can't bear to look at you! What will become of you? You'll never be yourself again. I know you won't . . . your face. Your lovely, lovely face . . . it's not there any more, is it? You can't say it will come back, Rob, because it won't. The doctor told me. I've spoken to him. I've spoken to your mother. I know, Rob. I know that you'll always be . . .'

'What? What will I always be? Me, that's what. Whatever I look like, whatever happens, I'll always be me underneath and I'll always love you.'

Millie stood there, tears streaming down her cheeks, but not looking at me. After a while she took out a hankie and blew her nose. She couldn't look at me. All the time she was in the room she stared at her feet, at the door, at my mother – anywhere but at me.

In the end she said, still with her eyes turned away, 'I'm so sorry, Rob. I really am. I'm more sorry and sad than I can say, but I have to go. I can't see you any more. I can't bear it . . . I can't bear to look at your face. I can't . . . I just . . . I'm so sorry, dear Rob, I just can't think of . . . Oh, Rob, please forgive me.'

She left then. I wanted to cry but I wasn't allowed to, because of the bandages. So I stifled my tears. I could feel them filling up the spaces in my head. If I tried to speak, if I opened my mouth, I imagined they would pour out of me like a stream.

I knew what Millie meant. She couldn't imagine what it would be like to kiss me. I was hideous. Her mouth . . . our mouths opening to one another – I spent hours imagining how that would be. And she, when she thought of the same thing, would be filled with nothing but horror.

Once I was out of hospital, I saw Millie from time to time, but she always crossed the road to avoid me.

Chapter Four

Captain Harry's ghost followed me home. I knew it would. I saw it mostly in the hall, standing by the hatstand. It looked like the captain – the same as ever, only not as solid. I tried to speak to it. I said, 'I will go and find them, Captain, I promise,' but as soon as I opened my mouth the ghost faded away, and I was left speaking to myself.

My mum caught me once, talking to the air.

'Who are you talking to?' she said, coming out of the kitchen with flour on her hands. 'I heard you talking.'

'To myself,' I said. 'I'm sorry.'

She gave me a funny look but didn't say anything. After that, if I glimpsed the captain's ghost in the house, I shut up. It kept mostly to the attic bedroom, where I still slept.

Mum had offered me the nice little bedroom looking out over our tiny garden, but I refused. I liked my attic. I felt safe there. Up in the space under the roof, I could lie on my bed and imagine that I was still good-looking. That Millie still might want to kiss me. I could pretend my face was the face I went to war with. In this room the captain was often in the small chair by the door, and I liked to see his shade sitting there. It never spoke to me, but I knew it wouldn't rest in peace till I'd found the family on the postcard.

I put the captain's Bible next to my old atlas on the bookshelf. Mum had kept that because I'd liked looking at the maps when I was a boy. I read a bit of the Bible last thing at night and stared at the postcard. If I was lucky, I dreamed about the family – Captain Harry looking brave in his uniform and his pretty wife and little girl. In the dream, I sometimes took tea with them, and Mrs Ashton would say, 'Have a cup of tea, Rob, do!' and hand me a white cup and saucer.

Those were the good nights. More often I would wake up sweating after a dream in which the noise of the guns filled my ears. Worst of all was seeing my dead friend Tom while I slept. I'd been to visit his mother and father when I got out of hospital. It was almost the first thing I did. I wish I hadn't.

I didn't know what to say to them. They didn't know what to say to me, but I could see what they were thinking. They thought I'd be better off dead, like Tom. They didn't say so, but I could tell.

When I got home, I wondered if they were right. Would it have been better if I'd died? I asked my mum and she was furious.

'What do you mean? Just because you're not handsome, not a matinee idol any longer, does that mean you can't enjoy things? Little things if you like, compared with what you had, but still. What about . . .' she hesitated, 'what about the trees and the flowers? Nice food. Books. You could read more now. You always liked a good book, didn't you? You could listen to music.'

She glared at me. 'And what about me? I love you, Rob, and you're a comfort and a joy to me whatever you look like. Think of me. How would I be if you were dead? It doesn't bear thinking about. So stop that nonsense. I don't want to hear another word about it. You're alive, and alive is how you'll stay.'

She was right, I suppose. Still, to me my life felt like a desert. Flowers, trees, food, music, books – they were all very well. I had no friends, though, and not much hope of getting any. I said so to my mum.

'Who'll want to step out with me, Mum? No one will ever want to marry me. I'll never have children. I'll be alone for ever.'

'You don't know what's in the future. What if Dr Hughes was right and your face can be . . .'

'Patched up,' I said.

'Well, that would be something, wouldn't it?'

'I'm not sure.'

Mum sighed and went on knitting.

'You need,' she said, 'to find some work.'

'Who'd have me?' I asked her.

'I don't know, but I am going to think about it. There's someone I can talk to.'

'Who?' I felt a bit annoyed. I didn't want to be taken on out of pity. I didn't want to see people flinching when they spoke to me. I wasn't sure if I wanted to talk to anyone. When I went out, I wore a hat with a wide brim and my coat collar turned up. I waited for the dark, mostly, because I could walk in the shadows. During the day, I kept to streets that were less busy. I was good at making myself disappear into the background.

There were many of us war-wounded in London. You saw us everywhere. Shining shoes. Selling newspapers near the underground. Tending barrows of fruit and veg in the market. There were blokes with no arms. They mostly wore their sleeves pinned up. Others had peg legs or eyepatches. When I saw someone else like me, wearing a mask, I turned away and walked back to where I'd come from.

One day, I went to look for the photographer. The one who'd taken the picture of Captain Harry and his family. I couldn't find any more excuses not to go. I took a bus. I found the street and walked up and down, looking for Kenton's. I found it at last and went in. The bell over the door rang as I stepped inside.

'Can I help you, sir?' said a woman with grey hair.

'Thank you,' I said. I was relieved to see that she didn't bat an eyelid when she saw my face. 'I hope you can.'

Chapter Five

'Thank you,' I said. 'This is Captain Harry Ashton and his family.' I took the photograph out of my breast pocket and laid it on the counter. 'It has your name on the back.'

The woman picked up the postcard. 'Yes,' she said. 'That's one of ours.' She laid it down on the counter again. 'But I'm afraid that my father – the photographer – passed away last year, and I don't remember this family. I'm so sorry. We're selling the studio. You've come just in time, really.'

I couldn't believe it. Was it possible that I'd never find the captain's family? I took a deep breath. 'Is there anyone – maybe a neighbour – who might remember them? They must have lived near here.'

'I could try my mother,' said the woman. 'Her memory is gone, mostly, but she might recall . . .'

The woman had a mother still living. She looked about sixty, so her mother would be ancient. Any hope I had was fading.

'Come with me,' she said. She lifted up a part of the counter and I followed her through to the back of the shop. It was like a museum in there.

'Don't mind the mess, sir,' the woman said. 'As I told you, we're packing up the studio.'

There were wicker tables and chairs stacked in one corner. Cardboard urns, bunches of flowers, rolled-up rugs, vases stuffed full of feathers and silk flowers stood about on the floor. There was a glass dome on one table. Under the glass, I could see wax apples and blossoms and a black bird with very shiny eyes. It looked at me and made me feel a bit funny. It was dead and not dead at the same time.

'This is my mother,' said the woman. 'Mrs Kenton the Elder. I'm Miss Kenton the Younger.'

I wasn't sure if this was a joke so I said nothing.

'Ma,' said Miss Kenton the Younger, 'this young man's brought a postcard in. One of ours. Do you know who this is?'

Mrs Kenton the Elder was tiny. A bit like the wax bird under the glass dome, her eyes were bright and black but she was very thin. Her hands, when she took hold of the postcard, were like the hands of a skeleton. You could see the bones of her skull under her skin. She had very little hair left.

She peered at the picture for a long time. I was ready to say goodbye and sorry for bothering them when she spoke.

'Harry Ashton,' she said. 'And Miss Kitty . . . what a pretty child. I can't remember his wife's name. Nice woman.'

'Yes!' I cried. I felt happiness, real happiness, for a moment. The kind of happiness I hadn't felt since 1914, since before I went to war.

If she knew their names, she might know where they lived. I hardly dared to hope.

'Thank you,' I said. 'Yes, it is my captain. Harry Ashton. He was killed in the war and I promised him I'd find his family.'

'You'll have a job,' said the old woman. Her voice was grating and thin, so quiet I could hardly hear what she was saying.

'Why?' Could she be right? Would I really not be able to find them?

'A bomb got their house – a Zeppelin raid,' said Mrs Kenton the Elder. 'They weren't hurt, though. That was very lucky. Everyone said.'

'But if they weren't hurt, why can't I find them?'

She looked at me then, and the light seemed

to have gone out of her eyes. She said nothing. Mrs Kenton the Younger touched me on the arm.

'Come out to the shop,' she said. 'She's gone back into silence. I can tell. It's like a candle flame, her mind. Her speech, too. It's there for a bit and then it goes away. But I remember that Zeppelin strike.'

We went back into the front of the shop. 'So you know what happened to Mrs Ashton and Kitty?'

'They moved. I know that.'

I hardly dared to ask the next question. 'Do you know their new address?'

'No, I'm so sorry. I have no idea. Everyone who was in that house left this area. That's all I know.'

I had to thank her for her help. I had to be polite and say how kind she and her mother had been. I said the words and left the shop as quickly as I could.

On the way to the bus stop, I realized something. The captain's daughter, Kitty, wouldn't be five years old any longer. She'd be about ten years old. She would look quite different. Maybe I wouldn't be able to recognize her. I could feel the hope that I'd carried in my heart for so long fading away.

Chapter Six

I had grown used to other people's reaction to me. When I stepped on to the bus on my way home, I didn't notice the little girl and a man who must have been her father. They were sitting in front of me, but the child turned as I sat down. She let out a sound between a scream and a sob.

'Papa! I don't want to see it! Papa, let's get off. There's a horrid man . . . look!'

She covered her face with her hands and her father tried to calm her. At the same time, he tried to say sorry to me. His face was bright red.

'He's not a horrid man, dear!' This was to his little girl. 'He's a soldier. He's been wounded. He'll be all better soon.' He turned round in his seat and said, 'I'm sorry, sir. Please forgive little Mary. She doesn't know . . . she's very young . . .'

'It's quite all right,' I said. 'I understand. No need for you to –'

He interrupted me. 'I was in France, too,' he said. 'You chaps were unlucky. I'm sorry for . . .' His voice faded away and he stared at me, his eyes fixed on my face. I stared back into his eyes and saw nothing in them but desperate misery. 'I have dreams,' he told me in a whisper, 'nearly every night.'

I nodded. The bus was far from my stop, but I had to get off.

'I wish you the very best of luck,' I said.

'And I wish you the same.'

I decided to walk the rest of the way home. I had to go over what I'd heard from Mrs Kenton and her daughter. As I walked, I was so deep in my own black thoughts that I noticed nothing. Perhaps people looked at me. I couldn't have cared less.

I was weeping now, quite openly, and I didn't mind who saw me. It didn't matter how long I turned things over in my mind, the outcome was the same. I would never, ever find the Ashtons. In a city like London, how could I know which street to look in?

I was in despair. Crossing over Putney Bridge, I looked down at the water. It was grey and muddy-looking. I watched it swirl around the pillars of the bridge. I could jump off the edge and drown myself. I would never have to feel pain again. My life could be ended in seconds.

I pushed myself away from the parapet. I could not do that to my mother. What had she said? 'You're alive, and alive is how you'll stay.' And Captain Harry . . . I'd be letting him down too. I'd promised to find his family, hadn't I? I went on walking.

As I came to our house, I glanced up at the front-bedroom window. The curtain moved and I could have sworn his ghost was there – the captain was looking out of the window. Waiting for me.

I shivered. This thin shadow of the man I once knew would be with me to the end of my life. Its presence would remind me of those dreadful times. I would never stop feeling guilt for my own failure to find his family. Looking for Kitty was out of the question, but I promised myself to look carefully at every woman's face I saw. I knew the truth, though. My chances of finding Mrs Ashton were about as good as my chances of picking out one particular grain on a long stretch of sandy beach.

Chapter Seven

There were certain things I did in the dark.

I needed the touch of someone's skin on mine. I needed someone not to turn away when I came near them. I wanted to be able to feel like any other young man. And I knew that there were women who would take money and be kind to those from whom most other women would shrink. They walked the streets round King's Cross. On evenings when things became too sad at home for me to bear, I would walk there as quickly as I could, keeping to the shadows as much as I could.

Netta, one of the women who took my money, was especially good to me. She wasn't pretty – not like Millie. I don't think she was as young as she pretended to be either, but she was full of laughter and smiles and my face didn't seem to matter to her. I asked her about it once.

'Doesn't it turn your stomach?' I asked her.

We sometimes lay on the bed for a while, after-wards, and chatted. 'My face, I mean.'

'I'm used to all sorts,' she answered. 'I like you. That's what matters. You're not one to rush off. You don't think I'm some kind of disgusting creature.'

I laughed. 'Why would I think such a thing? You're lovely.'

'Because what I do ain't respectable, is it? Doing what we just did for money? That's not nice, is it?'

I thought about that. 'I think,' I said, 'that what you do is kind.'

Netta sat up in bed. 'That's the best thing any-one's ever said to me. Thank you, darling.'

She leaned over and kissed me, properly. We hadn't kissed before. I had never tried to kiss her, which was funny, when you thought about it. Why did a kiss mean more than the other things we used to do? I don't know the answer to that, but it felt more private to me. More special. And now that Netta *had* kissed me, I felt privileged.

My times with her were like small lights in the long tunnel of my days. I told her so.

'You need to work, you do,' she said.

'That's what my mum says, too,' I told her. 'She's looking for something for me.'

'You'll be all right,' Netta said. 'You'll find something. Don't worry.'

At home, I did worry. I spent a lot of time reading. I learned bits of the Bible by heart, because I read them after I'd been looking at the postcard, night after night. I spent hours walking the streets. And I went to the Majestic as often as I could. Every time they changed the show, I was there.

I sat in the back row and let myself be taken away out of my own life and my troubles. When the lights went up, I came back into myself. It was like suddenly being pulled away from a warm and pleasant place. I was back in the dark, cold, real world. I had to go home. I had to leave the Majestic with its bright lights and red curtains and magical stories. I had to return to the shade of Captain Harry.

The ways I saw his ghost had changed. Now, I often fancied it was walking behind me. I felt his gaze on my back, day and night. At home, it kept to my room. When I sat down to take off my mask before I went to sleep, I could sense it sitting beside me. Sometimes, I even spoke to it.

'I can't do it, sir,' I'd say. 'I can't find them. I can't give them back your postcard. I wish I could but I can't. Please go away. Please rest in peace. Please, let me be.'

The captain faded a little, then, when I addressed him, but he soon came back. I wondered sometimes whether I ought to mention him to my mother, but I didn't want to scare her. She couldn't have seen him, ever, or she'd have told me. It's in my head, I told myself. In me – as much a part of me as my breath.

One evening, I was sitting at the back of the Majestic in my usual seat – on the side, by the aisle, and in the very back row. The dark fell over me and I felt – as I always felt when the lamps were dimmed – at peace. The faces and bodies of the actors up on the screen took over. I forgot who I was, what my troubles were, and turned my attention to their troubles, and their love affairs. Their lives lifted me out of my own.

I didn't notice anyone coming to sit beside me, but someone was there when the lights were turned on. He was a huge man, a little like the film actor Oliver Hardy. He was wearing a smart grey suit and held a hat on his lap. His shoes were shiny and black, and he had a grey moustache and a round bald head.

I must have looked startled because he said, 'Do not be alarmed, dear boy,' and I could hear that he had a foreign accent. 'My name is Oscar Brandywine.' He laughed and added, 'You're thinking it's a funny name, no?'

I was taken aback. What could I say? It was a funny name. I said, 'No, not at all.'

'I became Brandywine when the war began. It was a bad idea to have a German name in 1913 and 1914 . . . my name used to be Brandt but I changed it. I went for something a little more . . . well, a little more unusual.'

I didn't know why he'd started to speak to me. Why had he sat down in my row, next to me, when there were other seats nearer to the front?

He must have been reading my mind.

'You are thinking: why has this old man sat down next to me? Why has he started to talk to me?'

'Well . . .' I said and he waved his hand.

'Let me tell you what I've been thinking.'

Chapter Eight

At the end of the film we walked together into the foyer of the cinema. Mr Brandywine went first and I followed him.

'Come with me, please,' he said. 'I am the owner of this cinema and I have a small office here, though of course my main business is in the studio making films. Do you know about the studio?' he asked.

He was walking up a flight of stairs in front of me as he spoke and his words seemed to be floating down to me. I tried to answer him, but he went on talking and I found it hard to say anything. I nodded my head from time to time.

When we got to his office he waved a hand to tell me to sit down. His many papers and an inkwell were piled on an oak table. There were large photographs on the wall of the ladies and gentlemen who acted in the films I'd seen, and I gazed at them.

'You can close your mouth, young man,' he said and chuckled. 'You will meet many of these people, if you agree to what I'm going to suggest. They are only men and women, after all, like other men and women. I am the owner of the studio down the road and you will visit it, I'm sure. That is, if you're interested in seeing how the films are made.'

'I would be most interested.'

'Good, good. And then you will realize that, before the costume and make-up departments have worked their spells, the actors are quite ordinary, really. All of them.'

'They look better than most men and women I've seen,' I said.

'Well, that is true, I suppose, though you would be surprised at the magic powers of the camera. It can make us believe many things . . . Well now.' He went to his chair behind the table, sat down and clasped his hands together in front of him.

'I've been watching you,' he said. 'I saw you before the war, going in to see every show with a young lady. A pretty young lady. I don't see her any longer.'

Should I tell him about Millie? Was it any business of his? I said, 'She's no longer stepping out with me, I'm afraid. It's my face, you see.'

He sighed. 'Yes indeed. Your face . . . were it not for the war, I know you'd be as handsome as they are. I remember how good-looking you were.' He nodded towards the portraits on the wall, staring down at us like perfect dolls. Hardly like real people at all. 'But as it is, I can see . . . well, it can't be easy for you.'

'I'm used to it,' I said. That was a lie, but I didn't want him to feel sorry for me. I was tired of pity.

'Do you work?'

'No.'

'I thought not. I see you too often watching the films in the dark. Would you like to work? You don't, if you'll forgive me, look as if you are a rich young man.'

'I'm not. I would like nothing better than to work.'

'Have you thought of being a projectionist?'

'A what?' I had never heard the word before.

'One of the men who makes sure the films are shown properly. They feed the film on to reels, and then the light shines through the film and on to the screen. They make certain it all runs correctly. If they load the reels badly, you would get the story shown in the wrong order. Do you understand?'

I did. I said, 'I suppose I must have known

someone was in charge up there.' I'd often stared up at the opening on the back wall where the light shone through. You could almost see the images on the screen being carried along by the strong beams of light.

'That could be you,' Mr Brandywine said. 'How would you like that? You could share the work with Arnold, who's getting old now and would like a younger man he could teach. It'd be maybe three evenings a week and the afternoon show too, some days. Only a few shillings a week, of course, but it all mounts up. And there might be errands you can run for me in the studio.'

I could hardly believe what I was hearing. Mr Brandywine was offering me a job. A proper, regular job. A job, what's more, that I would love doing. I could watch every film for nothing. I could earn money in the dark. It sounded too good to be true. I said so to Mr Brandywine.

'Not at all,' he said. 'I knew you'd be just the person I have been looking for. You love the films. You are ashamed of how you look, though there's no reason for that. Well, I'm glad that's worked out so well. Can you start tomorrow?'

'Yes,' I said. I could hardly wait to tell my mother. 'Thank you.'

'Come at twelve o'clock. It's a matinee day,

and you can meet Arnold and he'll show you what to do. Till then, I'll bid you goodbye.'

My mother was very happy when I told her about my job. 'Oh, my dear boy,' she said. 'How kind he seems, this Mr Brandywine of yours. Funny name, though, isn't it?'

'He was born in Germany. He changed his name during the war, of course.'

She laughed. 'That's silly! Imagine! He had a chance to pick any name he wanted, and he went for Brandywine. He must be a funny fellow.'

'He is, rather, but kind-hearted.'

'Well, I've not been so pleased for a long time,' my mother said. 'I'm going to make sure your clothes are fit to be seen.'

She left the back parlour and I was alone. I could hear her in the kitchen, moving things around. I leaned back in my chair and closed my eyes. I knew, quite suddenly, that if I opened them, the captain would be there, nearby.

I was right. There he was, like a shadow, but pale, standing by the table. I hadn't seen him all day. I'd been busy. First I'd gone to the Majestic, and watched the film. Then I'd spoken to Mr Brandywine and on the way home, I'd been happy. It was a feeling I'd almost forgotten.

Also, I'd noticed that the captain came to me

for the most part in the dark and in my house. He didn't appear in the daylight on the street. Perhaps that was why I walked around so much. I often wished I had a shilling for every mile I walked.

But I knew why he was here now. He knew. He knew that if I took a job, I would think about his wife and daughter less. I would neglect my duty. I whispered, aloud, 'Don't worry, Captain. I'll keep looking. I promised you I would, and I will.'

My mother came in then. 'What are you sitting around here in the dark for? Light the lamps, for goodness' sake.'

I did so, but then I said to her, 'I'm going to step out for a while after supper, if you don't mind.'

'To the Star and Garter, is it?' she said, and I nodded. I'd made up the name of a public house. I'd told her that was where I went on the nights when I looked for Netta. I wanted to see Netta tonight. I wanted her arms around me. I wanted her to be happy for me. I wanted to be close to someone. Every bit of me needed her.

Chapter Nine

'So,' said Netta. She was sitting on the edge of the bed, pulling up her stockings. I lay back against the pillows. Netta's bed was not like mine. Her pillows were edged with lace. They smelled of her – a faint, sweet smell, which I loved. She turned to me and smiled. 'You're going to be up there, showing the films, then. That's a stroke of luck. Will you have time to come and see me?'

'Yes, Netta.' I rolled over and began to stroke her back. ''Course I will.'

I wanted to go on. I wanted to say: I think my feelings for you are what people mean by love, but I didn't dare. Netta was always kind to me. She made me feel as if she liked me. 'It's her job,' said a nasty voice inside my head. 'She's probably nice to all her punters.'

'You'd best be off, Rob,' she said. 'It's late, you know.'

It was. It was nearly midnight and I had been with Netta for two hours.

'I'm going,' I said. 'I'll get up now.' As I dressed, I said, 'I like this room so much. You've made it pretty.'

'Thank you.' She was at the dressing-table now, tidying her hair. 'I like it better than my own room at home.'

'Isn't this your home?'

'Bless you, of course it isn't! I rent this room from Ma Brown. She's a bit of a monster, but the rates are good and she's kind enough when you get to know her.'

'I would love it if you . . .' I couldn't go on.

'Love it if I what?' Netta asked, taking my hand.

'Will you come and meet my mama? You could come to tea.'

'Oh, my dear Rob!' Netta stood up and looked into my eyes. 'I can't do that, my pet. Don't you see that I can't?'

I said nothing.

Netta went on, 'She would know me at once for what I am. You can't see it, because you like me.'

'You're beautiful!' I burst out. 'I love you!'

There, the words were out at last and once I'd said them I felt better. Surely now Netta would see . . . She frowned.

'Rob, I'm a streetwalker. I go with men for money. I'm not respectable. And I'm not beautiful. You see me when I'm all done up. Your ma would have fifty fits if you took me home. And,' she said, as though this last thing was the most important, 'I'm practically old enough to be your mother.'

'You're not!' I burst out. 'I'm twenty-three.'

'And I'm thirty-eight,' she said. 'Too old for you by a long way.'

I was about to say more, to argue with her, but Netta hadn't finished.

'Come and sit down, Rob. I want to tell you something.'

We sat down together. The sheets and the silk bedcover were a mess. I thought back to why they were in such a state and began to tremble.

Netta took a deep breath. 'I haven't told you, my dear, because I saw no reason to, but I'm a married woman.'

I stared at her, unable to believe what I was hearing. How . . . why . . . how could a man allow his wife to do what Netta did? Or maybe he didn't know. Maybe she'd kept it secret from him.

'You're wondering about my Jim, aren't you? Do I love him? How can he let me do what I do . . .' She was silent for so long that

I wondered if I should say something. She was staring down at the carpet. But finally she lifted her face and I could see that her eyes were swimming with tears.

'I married Jim when I was very young. Then he was wounded early in the war and couldn't work any longer . . . not really. He lost his leg. We didn't know where the next penny was coming from.'

'But your family? Your parents . . .' And why, I was thinking, could Jim not change his work to something that didn't require both legs? There were many men who'd come back injured, and all of their wives hadn't taken to the streets. I began to hate this Jim with a passion. He must, I thought, be an unfeeling brute.

'They were far away, in the country,' Netta said. 'Then my mother died and Jim's father and there was no one. This . . .' she waved her hand to take in the room, its frills and its pretty lampshade and its silk bedcover, 'is what we decided to do. Jim had the idea.'

I was so astonished that my mouth fell open. Netta laughed, but there was no joy in her laughter.

'When you're choosing between starving and living really rather well, there's no choice.'

There were things I wanted to ask her. How

44

could Jim face her every day, knowing what he knew? I couldn't understand my own reaction to what she was saying. I was sad, because my dream of one day being with Netta all the time had gone for ever. And suddenly, I felt a jealousy towards this Jim that I'd never felt towards any of Netta's other men. She must love him, I thought. She wouldn't stay with him if she didn't.

Netta must have been reading my mind. She said, 'I don't love him. I suppose I couldn't do this if I loved him as other women love their husbands. He's cruel. If I don't earn enough to suit him, he stops speaking to me for days at a time.'

'Leave him,' I said. 'Come with me. Stay with me. I'll look after you. I won't mind if you're respectable or not. We'll run away. We'll go to another place. Another town.'

She shook her head. 'You've got a duty to your mother. I have a duty to Jim. I made vows when I married him. I can't break them and live with myself, however I feel about him. And you have a job. You're starting work, remember?'

I sat down on the bed, eaten up by feelings I couldn't control. Jealousy, sorrow, and a huge sense of being useless. You can't do anything right, I told myself. Everything you touch goes wrong. You'll never be happy.

'Don't feel so sorry for yourself,' Netta said. 'Chin up! You can still come and see me.'

'I will,' I said, 'though it won't be so often. Not now I'm working.'

'Never mind, my dear. Never mind. No point in weeping over what can't be changed, is there?'

Chapter Ten

I had learned never to weep. Tears would run down over my mask, but sometimes they fell between the mask and my skin and that was horrible. I walked home through the fog and felt sad, in spite of the new job awaiting me. The night seemed darker and colder than it had earlier, and I listened to the only sound in the silence – my own footsteps on the pavement.

I kept away from Netta over the next few weeks. I could not think of her without hating her husband, and hating myself for not being able to take her away from him. And did I love her? I no longer knew if I did. I needed her. That was certain, but I couldn't think of being with her without feelings of jealousy and anger rising in me.

Also, my new job made it easier not to think about Netta. There was so much to learn if I wanted to be a projectionist. How to set up the reels, how to stop and start the projector. How to check the reels were in the right order. Arnold was an elderly man with white whiskers. He didn't speak much, but I could tell it was nothing personal. He didn't mention my face. I don't know if he even saw it. He told me what I needed to know. He was very fussy about time-keeping, and made me promise I would never be late for my shift.

'It isn't me, mind,' he told me. 'It's them.' He pointed down to the people in the seats below us. 'They can't be kept waiting, can they? They've come for a two o'clock show, and a two o'clock show is what they must have. Not a quarter to three show. Or even a five past two show. You come in on time, young lad.'

'I will,' I said. And I did.

For the first few days, Arnold stayed with me while I went through all he'd taught me. After a while, he began to trust me. Then I was left to run the shows on my own. The day I ran the film by myself for the first time was a proud one for me.

Apart from coming in to show the films, I was given many tasks down the road in the studio where Mr Brandywine needed my help.

'They are getting some wigs in tomorrow,' he would say to me. 'Can you help with the unpacking?' Or, 'They need help with painting the backdrop. Do you think you could spare an hour?' Or, 'Mrs Freeman needs some costumes picking up from a shop in Covent Garden. Could you go?'

In this way, I found myself in the kinds of places I never thought I'd visit again – shops that reminded me of my first job at the draper's. I went to hat-makers, haberdashers, shoemakers. Into places where wigs were curled and trimmed, and to tiny shops full of boxes of beads and false jewels for sewing on to costumes. And no one in any of these places ever spoke about my face.

I loved the film studio. When I first went into it, I saw at once that this was where dreams were made. That was what a film was – a kind of dream. You could sit in the dark and imagine you were somewhere else. You could pretend the story you were watching – full of beauty and sunshine – was real life. The pretty ladies and handsome men on the screen were as genuine as could be.

In the studio, you could watch them making the magic. You could see everything changing under the gaze of the camera. The jewels, that looked cheap and too bright when they were being sewn on, became real diamonds when you were in the dark seeing them being worn by the stars on the screen.

I became used to everyone in the studio and they were used to me. I stopped being ashamed of my face. To tell the truth, there were days when I hardly thought of myself at all.

I stopped seeing Netta. I went to say goodbye to her one night, to try and explain my feelings. We didn't go to her room, but stood at the corner of the street, talking for a while. She said, 'You look after yourself, Rob. Don't stand in the shadows for ever. You're a lovely young man and don't you forget it.'

'And you're the kindest person I know.' I kissed her quickly before I turned to walk home.

At first, after our parting, I thought of her often, but in the end she became another small piece of a life I no longer recognized as mine. Would she miss me at all? Then I reminded myself that I was the one who loved her. She hadn't felt more than a kind of friendship for me, and perhaps pity too. There were nights when I was tempted to visit her. Then I remembered that we'd said our goodbyes, and I remembered her husband. The thought of him crushed the desire I had felt for Netta.

So I went from day to day, more content than I'd been for a long time. The ghost of Captain

Ashton never came to the Majestic. It kept to my bedroom. When I was there, all on my own, it would sometimes appear. My dreams were still full of the trenches. I woke up sobbing often, and the captain would be there, sitting on the end of my bed, pale and nearly transparent. He faded with the light, mostly. But I looked every night at the photograph of him and his wife and daughter.

'How can I find them?' I asked his ghost, but there was no answer. Even when the Bible was shut and on the shelf next to the atlas in my attic bedroom, I saw the postcard. I could sense the glow of the white lace on that blouse, and the child's white pinafore, hidden among the pages.

One day, I was walking from the front entrance of the studio to the costume department. I was carrying two hatboxes in my arms. The studio had many large spaces where the filming took place, but it also had many long corridors. I was making my way along one of these when I saw two young girls coming towards me.

As I passed them, I said, 'Good morning.'

What happened next was so shocking that I dropped the boxes and they sprang open.

One girl, the smaller one, stood in front of me. She was stiff with fear and screaming. Her friend, who was taller said, 'Stop it! Stop screaming. There's nothing to scream about. What's the matter with you?'

The younger girl calmed down after a few moments and tried to speak quietly to her friend, but I could hear what she said, 'It's him. The monster. I told you, Marie. I told you there was a monster here. I saw him before. I saw him at the Majestic.'

Marie turned to me. I didn't know what to do, but I knew I had to say something. 'I'm not a monster. My name is Rob Stone. I wear this mask because my face was very badly hurt in the war, that's all.'

'I'm sorry, sir,' said Marie. 'She's . . . well, I'm sorry.' She turned to her friend. 'Go on. Tell Mr Stone you're sorry too.'

'Sorry,' said the girl and then the two of them ran along the corridor towards the entrance.

I began to pick up the hatboxes. Who were these girls and what were they doing in the studio? Perhaps they were young actresses, needed for a film.

'What are you doing here, Stone?' said Mr Brandywine. He had popped out of one of the doors along the corridor.

'I . . . there were two little girls in the corridor and I startled them. I dropped the boxes, I'm afraid.'

'No harm done,' said Mr Brandywine. 'They are both very keen on seeing how we make the films. They are stage-struck, I suppose. The mother of the younger child is a friend of mine, so I said they could visit us and see how we work. I'm sorry if you were upset.'

'No, it was my fault. I wasn't upset in the least.'

That was a lie. I had forgotten what it was like to terrify someone. Time, and Netta's acceptance of me, and my new work had made me forget how I looked. This child had been rigid with fear. My face, the sight of me, still made children scream.

Chapter Eleven

One late afternoon in November I walked out of the Majestic after the matinee into a thick wall of fog. It was the kind of fog known as a pea-souper. People often say, when the fog comes down, that they can't see a hand held up in front of their face, but this time it was true. I couldn't see anything. The horrible, damp, yellowish stuff seemed to be pushing against my face. I had to feel about with my foot to find the steps down to the pavement.

I knew my way home. Of course I did, but how to tell which road was which? The street lamps were no more than misty glowing circles in the gloom. I would have to feel my way along the walls of shops and houses to be sure that I was going the right way.

Other people were shuffling along like ghosts too. I breathed in the fog, even though I had the woollen scarf Millie had knitted me around the lower part of my face. She'd sent it to France and I used to think of it as a token of her love for me. It was no longer that, of course, but it was the only good scarf I had. I'd stopped longing for Millie months ago.

I had only gone a few steps when I heard a child crying. I stopped and listened. Yes, someone was weeping. It sounded as though they were close to me, but I couldn't see anything. I didn't know where the sad noise was coming from. I called out, 'Hello? I can hear you crying . . . Where are you? Are you lost?'

More sobbing came to me through the dank foulness that hung in the air.

'Yes . . . Please help us. We can't find our way home.'

I knew that voice with its slight Irish accent.

'Is it Marie? I met you at the studio, didn't I? I'm Rob Stone. Do you remember me?'

'Yes!' Marie answered. 'Do you know the way to Grindley Street? That's where we're going. We know the way but we can't see where we are in the fog.'

'I do. I'll take you there. Where are you?'

I put my hands out in front of me and felt about. It was like moving through dirty cotton wool. At last I found Marie and her little friend. I didn't bend down to look at them, but grasped a small hand that waved at me in the gloom.

'I'll take you to Grindley Street,' I said.

'We do know the way. We've been to the Majestic so often. It wasn't foggy when we went in.'

'I know. Don't worry. It's very hard to find your way in a pea-souper.'

I held Marie's hand and she held the hand of the other little girl. She was the one who'd screamed when she saw me. What did she think now? For her, the fog might have been a blessing. She couldn't see my mask. I said, 'We won't be long now. This is Linden Grove.'

We walked along in silence for a while and then Marie spoke. She was clearly the kind of child who liked to talk rather than leave a silence. She would grow up to be a woman who was friendly to everyone. She said, 'Do you like being up there, at the Majestic?'

'Yes, I do. I like being in charge of showing the films.'

'I'd like that. I'd like to be the one who chose what films were on. I'd have more like *The Pirate's Bride*. That's my favourite.'

'I don't decide what films to show. Mr Brandywine does that. I just make sure the right film is there when people are waiting to see it. And that the reels are in the proper order.'

'Does it hurt, under your mask?' Marie asked.

I was taken aback. No one had asked me that since I'd left hospital. 'No, it doesn't really hurt very much any longer.'

A long silence fell. The fog muffled the sounds of the traffic, though you could hear the odd horse-drawn carriage clip-clopping down the road. Marie spoke up again. 'May I ask you something else?'

'Marie!' the other child said. It was the first time she'd spoken.

'He doesn't mind,' Marie said to her friend. 'Do you, Mr Stone?'

'No, I don't mind.' What was she about to ask? Perhaps I would mind, but it was too late to take back my words now.

She said, 'What do you look like underneath the mask?'

'Marie!' the other child squeaked. 'That's rude! How can you?'

'It's not rude,' I said. We were walking very slowly, feeling our way. I knew we were nearly at Grindley Street. Soon I would be knocking on a door and the girls would go inside and that would be that. But I had to answer. I'd said I didn't mind, and in one way I didn't. Of all the people I had met since being wounded in the war, young Marie was honest and curious and brave. I owed her an answer.

'My skin,' I said, 'looks very raw. Very red and sore. As if my whole face had been burned. It's not very nice. I'm glad of my mask. I know it looks strange, but I am sure that my face is even worse.'

We turned a corner. I said, 'Here we are. This is Grindley Street. What's the number of your house?'

'Twenty-six,' said the smaller girl. 'I live at number twenty-six. Marie is coming to tea at my house today.'

'That's good,' I said. I'd been glad to help the girls out of the fog, but I also wanted to be at home myself.

'Here it is. This is my house!' The smaller girl ran up to a big brass knocker in the shape of a lion's head. She banged it down hard. Then she did it again.

The door opened. A woman stood there, and the moment she saw the girl, she came forward and hugged her close.

'Oh, Kitty darling,' she said. 'And Marie! I was so worried. I was just coming to look for you both. The fog – it's so horrid.'

She looked at me. I was standing some way back from the door and the fog hid me a little.

'Mr Stone found us and brought us here,' said

Kitty. 'He works at the Majestic. I told you about him. Do you remember?'

'Oh, yes!' said the woman. I could guess what she had told her mother – how she'd met a man in the studio who had a mask on and who looked like a monster.

'You're very kind, sir,' the woman said. 'Do come in for a moment, so that I can thank you properly.'

I almost made my excuses, but the name Kitty rang in my ears. The same name as Captain Ashton's daughter. I stepped inside.

'You're most welcome, Mr Stone,' said the woman. 'My name is Edith Ashton.'

I must have stumbled, or fainted. I know that the next thing I felt was Mrs Ashton's hand on my arm. I was being led to a wooden bench in the hall, near a small table. The girls had gone. I think Mrs Ashton must have sent them away. I sat there, confused, full of wonder and amazement. This woman. The child Kitty. They were Captain Ashton's wife and daughter. The fog had led me to them. I stood up.

'I'm sorry. It was the shock of hearing your name. Are you the widow of Captain Harry Ashton?'

'Yes,' she said. 'I am. How do you know my late husband's name?'

'I was in his regiment. I was there when he died. And at home I have something of his that I must return to you.'

Now Mrs Ashton looked shocked. The colour left her face and she was almost as white as the captain's ghost. She sat down on the bench herself.

'Harry . . .' She got a grip on herself. 'I'm sorry. It's such a shock. I thought . . . I thought there was nothing left. You cannot know how alone I have felt. I thought everything was quite gone.'

'I'll bring it to you . . . what I have,' I said.

'Please do. Please come and have tea with us. Soon. Can you come tomorrow?'

'Yes, I could come to tea before I'm due at work in the evening. Thank you.'

There was nothing more to say. I left the house and made my way along Grindley Street. It was only when I'd turned into Linden Grove that I noticed that the fog was lifting.

Chapter Twelve

When I got home, I told my mother about my adventure in the fog. I told her about the captain's wife opening the door. She said, 'You deserve a medal, you do. I can't get over it. Of all the houses in London, you knock on that door. It's meant. That's what. The good Lord guided you to that door. Your guardian angel, maybe.'

I smiled. At any other time, I'd have said, 'Nonsense,' but it didn't feel like nonsense. Part of me agreed with my mother.

That night, I didn't sleep. I lay on my bed, holding the Bible. From time to time I took out the postcard. In a few hours I would give the book and the photograph to Mrs Ashton.

She had changed since it was taken. She looked thinner. Her hair was turning grey. Yesterday, she had been wearing a dark blouse with a high collar. There had been no lace at her cuffs. As for little Kitty, I could see, if I looked hard, that she was the girl I had met, but five years had passed. She was quite changed.

'I've found them,' I told the captain. When I looked up from the pages of his Bible, I could see him, but not as clearly as before. He was there, near the door. 'You can rest in peace. I'm going to tea at your wife's house tomorrow. I will give them your Bible. And your postcard.'

What I didn't say was, I will miss it. The Bible as much as the image of my captain in his uniform, looking brave and happy. I knew I could buy another Bible, but it would not be the same. This one had been in Captain Ashton's kitbag. Its cover was spotted and stained with the dirt of the Great War. Some of the pages had been torn. No other Bible would be the same. Still, it belonged by right to the captain's widow.

Going over the top. Leaving the safety of the trench to face the unknown. That's what it was like the next day when I walked down Grindley Street to number twenty-six. My heart was beating in my chest. I had dressed in my best suit and wore a clean shirt. I carried the Bible in my hand, wrapped in brown paper. My mother had made the parcel.

'You can't take the good book through the streets with nothing to cover it,' she'd said.

A woman I'd never seen before answered the door. I didn't know what to say. She looked a little like Mrs Ashton, but with golden curly hair pulled into a bun on the top of her head. She wore a blue and white striped blouse. The blue matched her eyes. She was smiling at me.

'You must be Rob Stone. Kitty and Edith are in the kitchen. They have just taken some biscuits out of the oven. Kitty wanted to make them for you. All by herself. Between you and me, I think Tilda, our maid, helped her a little. I'm Edith's sister. My name's Eliza Perkins. Do come in. Come into the front parlour.'

She went on talking as we walked across the hall. 'We hardly ever use the parlour, so this is a treat for us. Do sit down.'

I didn't know what to say. It didn't matter, because Eliza seemed happy to talk for both of us.

'I've come to stay with Edith. From the country. I love London. There is so much to see.'

'Yes,' I agreed. 'Though I don't see much of it these days. I work at the Majestic. In the projection box.'

'I know. I know all about you. Kitty told me how gallant you were yesterday. It was very kind of you to bring the girls home.'

'Not at all. Anyone would have done the same thing.'

'I'm not sure they would. Most people would want to go straight home on such a foggy night.'

Mrs Ashton and Kitty came into the room. A maid followed them, carrying a tea tray and a plate of biscuits. I stood up.

'How good to see you!' said Mrs Ashton.

Kitty ran up to me and said, 'Look at my biscuits. I made them for you. Will you eat one?'

'Yes,' I said. 'Of course I will.'

We all sat down. Mrs Ashton poured the tea. The Bible in its brown paper wrapping lay at my feet.

'Kitty, dear,' said her aunt Eliza, 'these biscuits are very good.'

'Yes, they are,' I said.

Kitty looked pleased.

I put my cup of tea down on its saucer. I cleared my throat.

'I've brought you Captain Ashton's Bible. Here.' I picked up the parcel and took it over to where Mrs Ashton was sitting. 'There's a photograph of the captain and of you and Kitty, too.'

Mrs Ashton's hands were trembling as she untied the string. She took the Bible and held it for a moment.

'Oh!' she said. 'It's so . . . battered.'

'It was with him in the trenches. The captain looked at your picture every day.'

She had found the postcard. Kitty went to her mother's chair and leaned over the arm. 'Let me see, Mama,' she said. 'Oh, look at me! How small I was! A baby.'

Mrs Ashton said nothing. She stroked the image of the captain with one finger. 'Harry . . .' she murmured. 'Oh, Harry! We were so young. He was so handsome. Wasn't he handsome?'

'He was. And a fine man, too. I . . .' What could I say? That the captain had saved my life with his care? That I would remember him for ever? That I'd loved him? In the end I said, 'He was the best of men. We all . . . he helped every one of us. To survive. To get through it. I miss him.'

'Yes,' said Mrs Ashton. 'I miss him very much too.' Kitty had left the room. She had gone to fetch Polly, the doll who was on the chair in the photograph.

'Can you tell me how he died? While Kitty isn't here? I don't want her to hear it, but I want to know.'

'A mortar shell. He died at once. He wouldn't have known about it. It was over before you could blink. He didn't suffer. Not for a second.'

That was true. I said no more. I didn't tell her how it was to see someone blown apart.

She said, 'Thank you. I'm glad of that at least.'

I went to sit down again. I picked up my cup. Kitty came back with the doll.

'I don't play with her now,' she said. 'I'm too old. But she sits on my bed.'

'She's very pretty,' I said.

We went on talking. It was mostly Eliza who spoke. She was someone who said what came into her head. She looked hard at me. 'I'm sorry to stare, but I'm most interested in your mask. There is such good progress being made now. To fix the damage to skin. I've heard so much about the work of the surgeons in some hospitals. Will you be getting the new skin grafts?'

Mrs Ashton looked up. 'Eliza! You hardly know Mr Stone.'

'Rob. Please call me Rob. All of you. I don't mind the questions.'

How could I tell them? Eliza was the first person I'd met since I was wounded who had looked me straight in the eye. She had met my gaze from the moment she opened the door. My mask did not repel her. She didn't mind how I looked. Why should she care? I said to myself. I will probably never see her again. She would go back to the country and that would be that.

'I'm sorry, Rob,' she said to me. I liked her

smile. It lit up her face. 'I'm going to train to be a nurse. That's why I'm living with my sister.'

I nodded. That was why she could face me so bravely. It would not have done for a nurse to be squeamish.

'I'm sure you'll be a very good nurse,' I said. I meant it. I could imagine Eliza walking between rows of beds and smiling at the sick people.

The talk became more general. Eliza liked reading.

'What's your favourite novel?' she asked me.

'Eliza, Rob hasn't said he likes reading.'

'I don't read as much as I'd like to,' I said. That was true. I made up my mind in that moment to read a great deal more.

'Have you read *A Christmas Carol* by Charles Dickens?' she asked.

'Yes,' I said, thanking my lucky stars that she had chosen a book we had read at school. 'It was . . . I liked it very much.'

'My favourite novel is *Jane Eyre* by Charlotte Brontë. What do you think of it?' Eliza's eyes shone.

'I've not read it,' I answered.

'Then I shall lend it to you,' she said and left the room to fetch it.

'You don't *have* to borrow it,' said Mrs Ashton. 'Eliza does get carried away.'

'No, I'd be glad to read it. If she likes it so much, then it must be good.'

'You may not enjoy it. You may not share Eliza's taste.'

'I will know when I've tried it,' I said.

Eliza showed me to the door when I left. I held her copy of *Jane Eyre* in my hand.

'Goodbye,' I said. 'And thank you.'

'It's been good to meet you. I will see you again when you bring back my book. We can talk about it.'

'Yes,' I said. 'I look forward to that.'

As I walked down Grindley Street, I almost burst out laughing. If only Eliza knew! The need to bring back the book and see her again was the main reason I'd been so keen to borrow it.

Chapter Thirteen

All the way home, I thought about Eliza. In my hand, the book was heavy. I could take it back to her, but not before I'd read it. I wished I could see her more quickly. It would take me weeks of reading to finish *Jane Eyre*. I made up my mind to read in every spare moment.

Eliza wasn't truly pretty; not in the way Millie had been. She was dressed plainly. Her face was scrubbed and clean, and her skin was pale and clear. Netta's powdered face came into my mind. Netta's red lips were nothing like Eliza's. Netta's perfume was heavy and sweet. Eliza smelled of a flowery field.

None of this mattered. Eliza spoke to me as if we were equals, as if we were friends. She wanted to speak to me. And she did not flinch when she looked at me.

When I reached my bedroom, I lay on the bed and opened Eliza's book. 'There was no possibility of taking a walk that day . . .' the novel began. I read on, pleased to hear the voice of a young girl in my head as I turned the pages. I imagined Jane Eyre's voice to be very like Eliza's. The time passed happily.

When I looked up, I noticed something about my room. It was as though it had been cleaned. Had my mother been tidying? Scrubbing my floor? I gazed at my chest of drawers. I saw the jug and basin on top of it. I saw my books on the shelf. The rag rug by the bed looked the same as it always did. But the room was different. The gas light reached into the corners. I sat on the edge of the bed, feeling happy.

Then I knew what it was – Captain Ashton was gone. I wanted to speak aloud to him, as I sometimes did, but I knew he was no longer with me. I had done what I'd promised him I'd do. I'd found his family. Now, he would rest in peace for ever.

I went downstairs to join my mother for supper. There was no sign of the ghost. It was as if a blanket that had been lying on the house for a very long time had been lifted.

'I hope you're hungry,' my mother said. 'I've got some lovely chops for you.'

Eliza came to the Majestic. She and Mrs Ashton and Kitty were there to see the latest film. It was called *Summer Song*. Mr Brandywine was very proud of this film and had told me that he was sure the ladies would love it. I hadn't noticed them during the show, but I met them outside when I left work.

'Hello, Mr Stone!' cried Kitty. 'I said we must wait for you.'

'Thank you. Very good of you,' I said. I was surprised to see them. Eliza was smiling and Mrs Ashton seemed pleased.

She said, 'Walk along with us and take a cup of tea. There's something I've been meaning to ask you.'

'That's very kind. I'd love to.'

We walked along together. Mrs Ashton and Kitty fell back a little. Eliza and I were left together.

'Are you reading *Jane Eyre*?' she asked me. 'Do you like it?'

'I do,' I said. 'It's very . . .' I couldn't find the right word.

'Thrilling,' Eliza suggested. 'Moving. Frightening.'

'Yes.' I nodded. 'But mainly, I like Jane. I want to know what happens to her. I hope she will be happy at the end of the book.'

'Yes! That's it. You're quite right.'

I felt pleased by her praise.

'Here we are,' said Mrs Ashton as we came up the path to the door of twenty-six Grindley Road. 'Come in. I think Tilda has made scones.'

The scones were very good. We ate them with jam and cream.

Eliza and I talked. Or rather Eliza talked and I listened. She was interested in many things. Of course, she believed in votes for women. And she wanted to see Kew Gardens.

'Will you take me, Rob? I don't want to go on my own.'

I put my cup down. She struck me as very modern. I had never met a young lady who had so many ideas. Or, apart from Millie, a young lady who didn't wait to be invited to step out. I said, 'I would like to take you there very much.'

She smiled. 'Then it's decided. Are you working on Saturday?'

'Not this week,' I said. 'But Kew Gardens would be much nicer in the spring.'

'I'm sure there is much to see at any time,' Eliza said. 'We can go now and then again in spring.'

She thought we would still be talking to each other in the spring. She had given me a shining future. I didn't know what to say. She smiled.

'Cat got your tongue?'

'No, no . . .' I took a deep breath. 'Of course

we can go again in the spring. I'm looking forward to Saturday.'

'I'll ask Tilda if she'll prepare a picnic. What fun!'

Mrs Ashton stood up. 'Rob, would you carry the tray into the kitchen for me? Eliza, you wait here with Kitty, please.'

'Of course,' I said. What could she want to say to me? Me and Eliza . . . our friendship . . . was that worrying her?

I followed her and put the tray down on the kitchen table.

'Sit down, Rob,' she said, 'and don't look so worried.'

'I feel you might be angry with me.'

'Not at all. Not in the least,' she said and smiled at me. 'It's good that you and Eliza seem to be . . . well. That's not what I want to talk to you about.'

I waited. Mrs Ashton's hands were in her lap. She twisted them together. She said, 'Please do not think I have taken leave of my senses, but I would like you to tell me something.'

'Anything.'

'Do you believe in ghosts, Rob?'

'Yes,' I said. 'I have seen . . .'

'What have you seen? Tell me! Please tell me.'

How to begin? I took a deep breath. 'The

captain . . . I used to see the captain. Since he died, I've seen him many times. I don't see him any longer. I think he's at peace now. I promised him to return that postcard to you. Now that I have, he's gone. He's left me.'

'Well, lately I have begun to see . . . I have started to think . . .' She looked directly into my eyes. 'I think I see my Harry sometimes. In the dusk. At night. I think I see him standing at the end of my bed. I feel . . . I feel he's come back to me. To watch over me. Do you think I'm mad?'

'No, not at all. You're . . .'

'I feel less lonely, now that I can see him. I feel . . . well, I wouldn't say it to anyone else. But I know I can tell you. I feel he's come back to me. I'm comforted. I used to go to someone. I've never told anyone this, but I visited a medium and asked her if Harry had a message for me. From beyond the grave. So silly . . . as if those things could ever be true. But you do hear strange stories, don't you? I never believed them. But I had to give Harry a chance. To get in touch with me. Don't tell Eliza. She would think badly of me. She is so sensible. But since the early days, I haven't stopped looking for him.'

'I'm glad,' I said. 'The captain would want you to be happy. You know, he would.'

'I'm a great deal happier now that I've seen

him,' said Mrs Ashton. 'Thank you for bringing him back to me.'

She stood up. 'We'll say nothing, Rob. Do you agree to keep this private between us?'

'Of course. I won't say a word.'

'Then let us go and find the others.'

Chapter Fourteen

Eliza and I went to Kew Gardens on a bright, sunny winter's day. The sky was blue and I couldn't see a cloud anywhere. The air was cold. The breath came out of our mouths like smoke. We walked along the paths. Many trees had lost their leaves.

'I like the trees when they're bare,' Eliza said. 'The branches look like black lace on the blue.'

What she said was true. We looked at the tropical plants in the glasshouse. We sat on a bench. She asked me about *Jane Eyre.*

'Have you finished it yet?'

'Not long to go. I hope Jane doesn't marry St John Rivers.'

Eliza laughed. 'Wait and see.' She turned to look at me.

'Have you thought more about your face?'

'What do you mean?' For a moment, it seemed as though a shadow had fallen over the day. My face was the last thing I wanted to think about. When I was with Eliza, I liked to pretend I was like every other young man. I wanted everyone to think we were walking out together. But Eliza didn't like pretending. Eliza looked at life as it was.

'I think you should return to your doctors. I think it's time to try and restore your face.'

I thought of pain. I thought of doctors cutting me. Stitching me together again. More pain-killing drugs, more morphine. More suffering. More work for my mother in looking after me. More lying in bed in a ward filled with other suffering men.

'I'm frightened,' I said to her. 'It's so . . .'

'I'll help you,' she said. 'I'll come and see you often. I'll help to look after you when you come out of hospital. It will be good nursing practice for me.'

She tried to smile, to make light of the work this would mean to her.

'Why?' I asked. 'Why would you want to do so much for me?'

'Oh, Rob, you are a very slow person in some ways. Because I like you. Because I want you to be able to take off the mask.'

'The mask frightens some people, but it's not as bad as my real face would be,' I said.

'You don't know that,' Eliza said. 'You may be surprised at how much can be done. Please go and see the doctors. Will you promise me that? See what they say about your chances.'

'I'll do it for you,' I said.

Eliza stood up and pulled me to my feet. 'Good! I'll come with you if I can.'

We went on walking till the sun began to sink towards the horizon. A scarlet sunset spread through the sky. As dusk fell, Eliza shivered.

'It's getting very chilly now,' she said. 'Let's go home, Rob.'

I put my arm around her shoulders and she leaned against me as we made our way out of the garden.

Discover the pleasure of reading with Galaxy®

Curled up on the sofa,
Sunday morning in pyjamas,
just before bed,
in the bath or
on the way to work?

Wherever, whenever,
you can escape
with a good book!

So go on...
indulge yourself with
a good read and the
smooth taste of
Galaxy® chocolate.

Proudly supports

Quick Reads are brilliant short new books written by bestselling writers to help people discover the joys of reading for pleasure.

Find out more at **www.quickreads.org.uk**

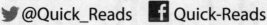 @Quick_Reads   Quick-Reads

We would like to thank all our funders:

   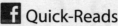   

LOTTERY FUNDED

We would also like to thank all our partners in the Quick Reads project for their help and support: NIACE, unionlearn, National Book Tokens, The Reading Agency, National Literacy Trust, Welsh Books Council, The Big Plus Scotland, DELNI, NALA

At Quick Reads, World Book Day and World Book Night we want to encourage everyone in the UK and Ireland to read more and discover the joy of books.

World Book Day is on 5 March 2015
Find out more at **www.worldbookday.com**

World Book Night is on 23 April 2015
Find out more at **www.worldbooknight.org**

Start a new chapter

Red for Revenge

Fanny Blake

Two women, one man: code red for revenge...

Maggie is married with two grown-up children.
Her twenty-five year-old marriage
to Phil has lost its sparkle.

Carla is widowed. She understands life is short
so she lives it to the full. But is her new romance
all that it seems?

When the two women meet in the beauty salon,
they soon find they have more in common
than the colour of their nails.

The discovery that they are sharing the same
man is shocking. How will Phil be taught
a lesson or two he won't forget?

Orion

Start a new chapter

Dead Man Talking

Roddy Doyle

Pat had been best friends with Joe Murphy
since they were kids. But five years ago
they had a fight. A big one, and they haven't
spoken since – till the day before Joe's funeral.
What? On the day before his funeral
Joe would be dead, wouldn't he?
Yes, he would...

Jonathan Cape

Start a new chapter

Paris for One

Jojo Moyes

Nell is twenty-six and has never been to Paris.
She has never even been on a weekend away with
her boyfriend. Everyone knows she is just
not the adventurous type.

But, when her boyfriend doesn't turn up
for their romantic mini-break, Nell has the
chance to prove everyone wrong.

Alone in Paris, Nell meets the mysterious moped
riding Fabien and his group of care free friends.

Could this turn out to be the most
adventurous weekend of her life?

Michael Joseph

Start a new chapter

Street Cat Bob

James Bowen

When James Bowen found an injured street cat
in the hallway of his sheltered housing, he had no
idea just how much his life was about to change.
James had been living on the streets of London
and the last thing he needed was a pet.

Yet James couldn't resist the clever tom cat,
whom he quickly named Bob. Soon the two were
best friends, and their funny and sometimes dangerous
adventures would change both their lives, slowly
healing the scars of each other's troubled pasts.

Street Cat Bob is a moving and uplifting story
that will touch the heart of anyone who reads it.

Hodder & Stoughton

Start a new chapter

Pictures Or It Didn't Happen

Sophie Hannah

Would you trust a complete stranger?

After Chloe and her daughter Freya are rescued
from disaster by a man who seems too good to be
true, Chloe decides she must find him to thank him.
But instead of meeting her knight in shining armour,
she comes across a woman called Nadine Caspian
who warns her to stay well away from him. The man
is dangerous, Nadine claims, and a compulsive liar.

Chloe knows that the sensible choice would be
to walk away, but she is too curious. What could
Nadine have meant? And can Chloe find out the truth
without putting herself and her daughter in danger?

Hodder & Stoughton

Why not start a reading group?

If you have enjoyed this book, why not share your next Quick Read with friends, colleagues, or neighbours.

A reading group is a great way to get the most out of a book and is easy to arrange. All you need is a group of people, a place to meet and a date and time that works for everyone.

Use the first meeting to decide which book to read first and how the group will operate. Conversation doesn't have to stick rigidly to the book. Here are some suggested themes for discussions:

- How important was the plot?

- What messages are in the book?

- Discuss the characters – were they believable and could you relate to them?

- How important was the setting to the story?

- Are the themes timeless?

- Personal reactions – what did you like or not like about the book?

There is a free toolkit with lots of ideas to help you run a Quick Reads reading group at **www.quickreads.org.uk**

Share your experiences of your group on Twitter 🐦 @Quick_Reads

For more ideas, offers and groups to join visit Reading Groups for Everyone at **www.readingagency.org.uk/readinggroups**

Other resources

Enjoy this book?

Find out about all the others at **www.quickreads.org.uk**

For Quick Reads audio clips as well as videos
and ideas to help you enjoy reading visit the
BBC's Skillswise website **www.bbc.co.uk/quickreads**

Join the Reading Agency's Six Book Challenge at
www.readingagency.org.uk/sixbookchallenge

Find more books for new readers at
www.newisland.ie
www.barringtonstoke.co.uk

Free courses to develop your skills are available in your
local area. To find out more phone 0800 100 900.

For more information on developing your skills
in Scotland visit **www.thebigplus.com**

Want to read more? Join your local library. You can borrow
books for free and take part in inspiring reading activities.